Dear Mom,
Your stories remain…

Tailor and Mischievous Mouse by Preeti Gulati

Published by: www.storiesbymymom.com

Copyright © 2023 Preeti Gulati

 For permissions contact: preeti@storiesbymymom.com

Cover and Illustrations designed by Anjali Shekhawat

ISBN: 979-8-9871087-1-0

First Edition

Tailor and Mischievous Mouse

The fancies of a little mouse
With a tailor next to his house

Bedazzled by a red sequin fabric
To look stunning like a Maverick.

He demanded a beautiful shiny hat
and pleased the tailor with a little chat.

He asked if it was ready yet?
If not, he made quite a threat!

"Quietly! At night I will swing
An army of mice I will bring

All your clothes we will nibble
and enjoy the sight with a giggle!"

His naughty singing, he thought was fun
Truly intended was all the pun.

This made the tailor worried and scared
He made a promise, the hat will be prepared.

Thinking he was king of the town
Mouse made everyone wear a frown.

Poor tailor made the shiny hat
Looking nice was the little brat.

Just when the tailor had done his best
There came another greedy request.

Shiny red booties I want this time
To look cool when I would climb.

"Leave me alone!" the tailor snapped
Yet another threat found him trapped!

"Quietly! At night I will swing
An army of mice I will bring

All your clothes we will nibble
and enjoy the sight with a giggle!"

Sluggishly, the tailor gave in
Ah! The mouse would have another win.

The shiny booties looked so awesome
For the mouse to shine and blossom.

Now his dreams knew no bounds
Mischief and greed were his surrounds

To have a taste of pride and success
He went to the palace to marry a princess.

The palace guards knew without a doubt
and showed the mouse a permanent way out.

No threats would work anymore
Harsh as it was, he was shown out the door.

Shooed were the fancies of the mouse
Left alone in the streets to browse

Leaving him a total wreck
Truly! It was a reality check.

Greedy as they were his crazy dreams
Not one worked of his naughty schemes.

A tough lesson did the mouse learn
Never be greedy, or the tables will turn.

"Dream big" did the tailor say
"But never go about it the wrong way!"

Author's note

A childhood would be incomplete without listening to stories from your mother. These stories take you to a special place. A world where anything is possible! Characters come to life in every shape and form. Some stories have a moral, while others just funny as they are. Some are about the mundane, others about the simple human emotions. Some rooted in a mystical world while others purely a work of fiction.

Tailor and Mischievous Mouse brings to life one such story by my mom. Originally recited in Hindi, this book is a rendition of the story in the form of a rhyme adapted to current context.

I look forward to bringing to you a collection of books with such timeless stories. Stories that will bring out a myriad of emotions - sometimes happy, excited at other times and yet at other times filled with curiosity.

You can visit me at storiesbymymom.com

Preeti

Ingram Content Group UK Ltd.
Milton Keynes UK
UKHW050135120523
421622UK00002B/16